The THREE BILLY GOATS FLUFF

Rachael Mortimer

Illustrated by Liz Pichon

Hodder
Children's
Books

Trip-trap

Trip-trap

Trip-trap

How was he supposed to sleep? Mr Troll buried his head in his pillow and groaned.

He looked back at the newspaper advertisement.
How could he have been so stupid?

TROLL PARADISE

FINE RIVERSIDE APARTMENT
WITH SLIMY TOADS AND
RUNNING BEETLE JUICE.
BARGAIN!

GREAT PAD
FOR SALE!

Something had to be done because what the advertisement had NOT said was:

WHOLE HOUSE AVAIABLE

NOISY!
UNDERNEATH THE ONLY BRIDGE FROM THE ROCKY MOUNTAIN TO THE LUSH GREEN FIELD.

A ROOM WITH A RUBBISH VIEW

For on the mountain next to Mr Troll's bridge lived the three Billy Goats Fluff. They loved to eat the lush green grass in the field by the bridge. It made their fleeces extra fluffy, important for Mother Goat's knitting business.

The three Billy Goats Fluff crossed the bridge twice a day.

But this morning, Mr Troll had a surprise for them. He'd put up a notice:

Little Billy Goat Fluff had not yet learned to read,
so he set off as usual. He'd just put one hoof
on the bridge when Mr Troll leapt out!

'I'm a Troll with
a very sore head.
Stop trip-trapping
over my bed!
When I'm tired and feeling blue,
There's nothing quite like
little goat stew!'

Little Billy Goat was very scared
and scampered back to Mother Goat.

Next came Middle-sized Billy Goat Fluff.
His hooves were louder than Little Billy Goat's.
Mr Troll leapt out again!

'I'm a Troll
in a very
bad mood.

Waking me up
is terribly rude!
Middle-sized goat makes
a lovely roast.
Or tasty pâté upon
my toast!'

Middle-sized Billy Goat raced
back to Big Billy Goat and
they were both too scared
to cross the bridge.
'We'll tell our mum about you!' they shouted.

Mother Goat listened to her Billy Goats and she thought about Mr Troll. She knew what it was like to live without sleep; Little Billy Goat still woke her up every night!

That night as she sat knitting booties from the finest Billy Goat Fluff, Mother Goat had an idea…

The next day Mr Troll was waiting for them!

'I'm a troll as tired as can be, I'm going to have goat and mash for my tea!'

Big Billy Goat Fluff trembled
as he handed Mr Troll
a note and a present
from Mother Goat.

If you can hear us trip-trap by
Then you can make three Billy Goat pie.
But if we're quiet as tiny mice
You must stop being grumpy and
start being nice.

Little Billy Goat Fluff was the first to try out Mother Goat's plan. He shakily put on the hand-knitted hoof muffs. They were so fluffy. Bright yellow. His favourite colour!

Slowly, he stepped out onto the bridge. Mr Troll
listened from his bedroom. Nothing?
Nothing!

Middle-sized Billy Goat Fluff was next.
His hooves were quaking as he put on four
exceedingly fluffy hoof muffs. Pink! Middle-sized
Billy Goat was a real softie.

Carefully, he stepped out onto the bridge.
Mr Troll had his ear pressed to the roof.
He couldn't hear a thing!

Finally, it was Big Billy Goat Fluff's turn. His hoof muffs had taken most of the night to knit. With four huge pompoms on his hooves, Big Billy Goat stepped onto the bridge.

Mr Troll strained his ears.
Silence at last!
How had they
done it?

Mr Troll came out from under the bridge. He looked at the three Billy Goats Fluff tucking into the lush green grass in the field. He looked at his present from Mother Goat. Then he opened it.

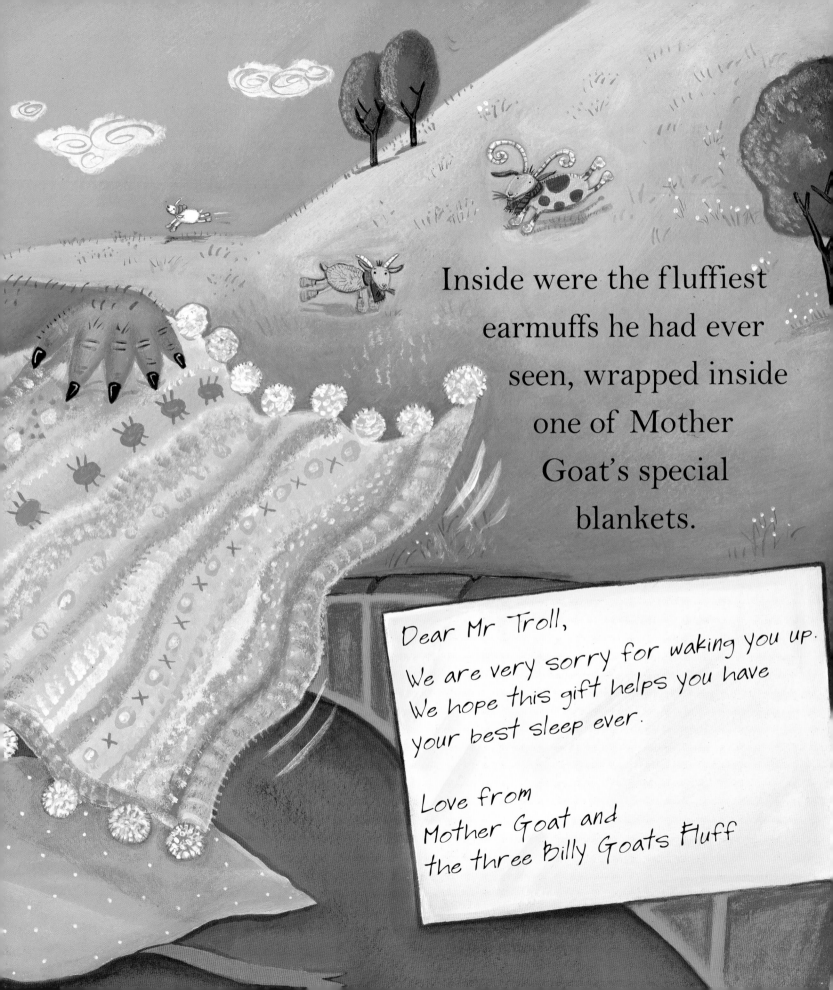

Inside were the fluffiest earmuffs he had ever seen, wrapped inside one of Mother Goat's special blankets.

Dear Mr Troll,
We are very sorry for waking you up.
We hope this gift helps you have your best sleep ever.

Love from
Mother Goat and
the three Billy Goats Fluff

That night Mr Troll
drank a hot mug
of beetle juice.

He read his favourite
bedtime story.

The Princess
and the Troll

TroLL

Then he put on his fluffy earmuffs
and cuddled his soft green blanket.

For the first time in his new house he slept and slept. He dreamed of fluffy clouds, fluffy toads, fluffy beetle juice and, best of all, his new quiet friends…

...the three Billy Goats Fluff!